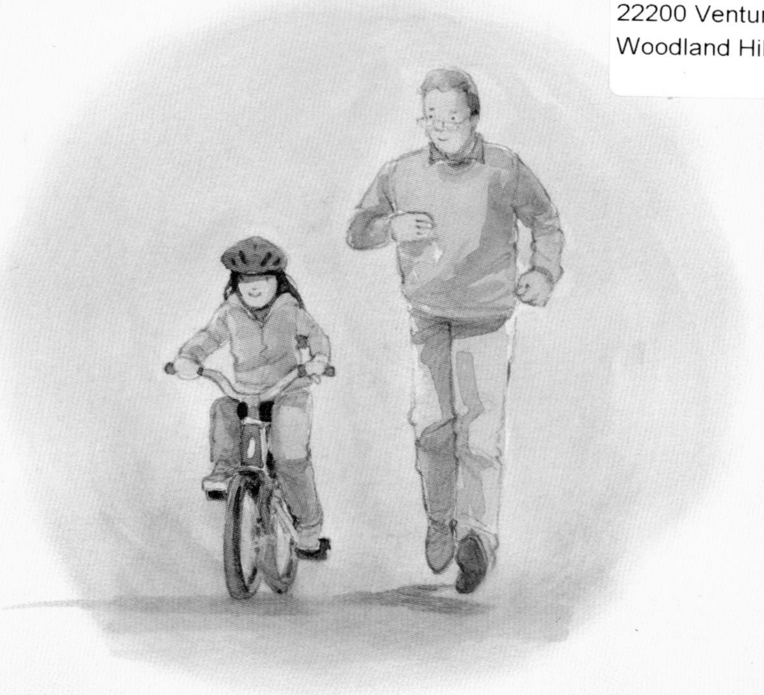

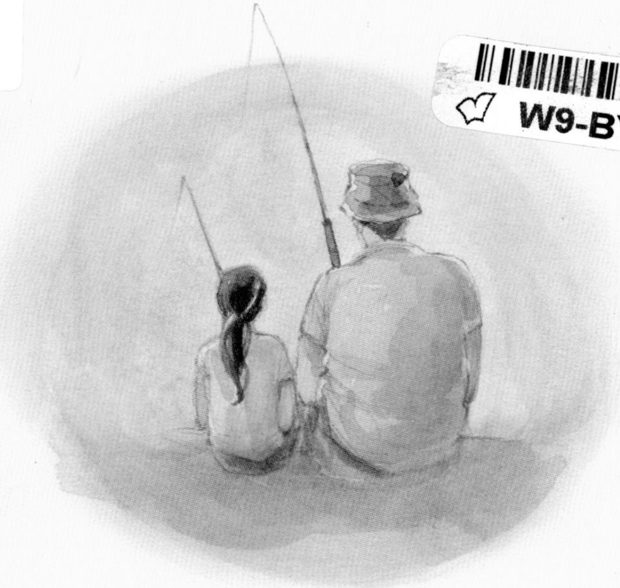

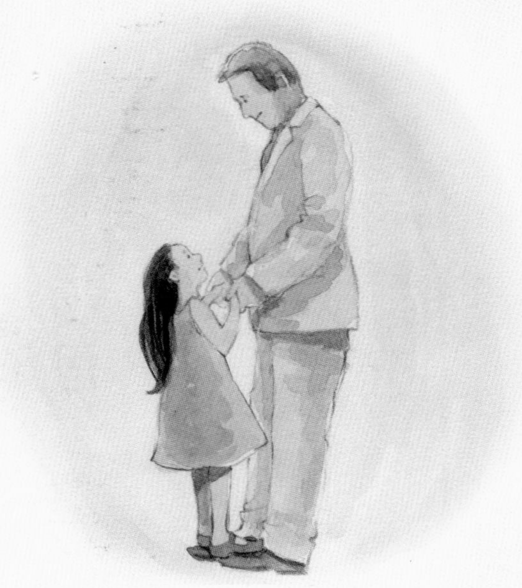

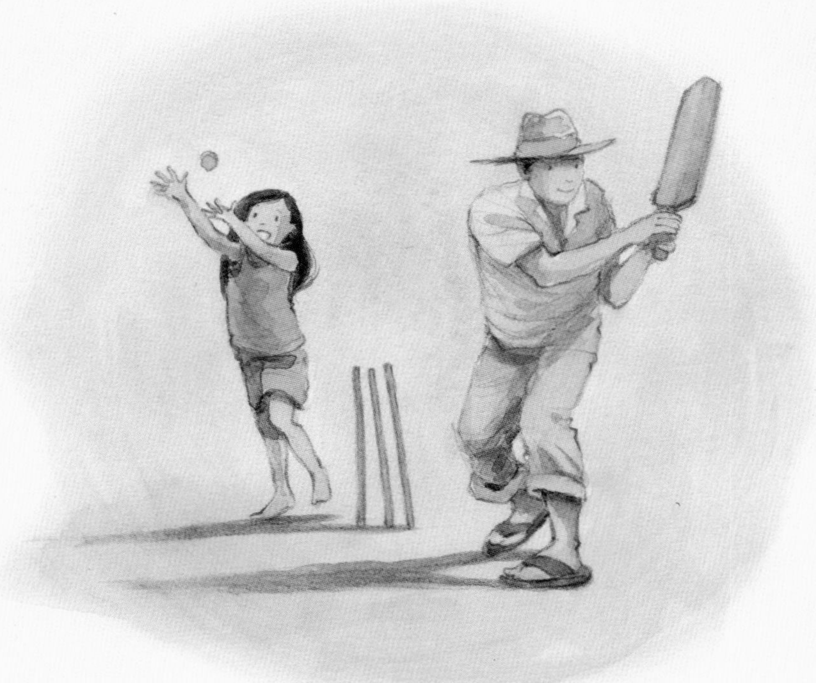

My Grandfather's War

GLYN HARPER & JENNY COOPER

First published 2018

EK Books
an imprint of Exisle Publishing Ltd
226 High Street, Dunedin, 9016, New Zealand
PO Box 864, Chatswood, NSW 2057, Australia
www.ekbooks.org

A CiP record for this book is available from the
National Library of New Zealand.

ISBN 978-1-77559-299-0

This publication is adapted from Glyn Harper's original text,
My Grandfather's War, first published by Reed Publishing (NZ)
Ltd in 2007.

Designed by Mark Thacker, Big Cat Design
Typeset in Historical Fell Type Roman 17 on 23pt
Printed in China

This book uses paper sourced under ISO 14001 guidelines
from well-managed forests and other controlled sources.

10 9 8 7 6 5 4 3 2 1

This is my Grandfather.

He came to live with us
just after I was born.
I call him 'Grandpa' but
his real name is Robert.

My name is Sarah and I am eight years old.
I go to the school just down the road.

Grandpa takes me to school in the mornings
and meets me when school is finished.

When we get home, Grandpa always gives me something to eat and we talk about what I did at school.

Then I do my homework. If it's too hard sometimes Grandpa helps me with it.

If I don't have any homework Grandpa will read me a story or sometimes we make things together.

There is something unusual about
my grandfather though.

He walks with a limp because
he hurt his leg a long time ago.

And sometimes he gets very sad.

My dad told me it was because
Grandpa had been to a war in
a place called Vietnam.

He told me never to ask Grandpa
about the war and to leave him
alone when he gets sad.

This made me want to find
out about Vietnam and the war there.

I could not find a book on the war
in Vietnam in our school library.

In the end I decided there was only one thing to
do. I would have to ask Grandpa about his war.

I did it one day after school.

We were having a glass of milk and sharing an apple when I asked him.

'Grandpa,' I said when I had finished eating my half of the apple.

'Yes, Sarah.'

'I want to ask you a big question, but I'm scared.'

He looked at me with concern.

'Grandpa,' I said quietly, 'why did you go to a war in Vietnam?'

Grandpa looked surprised. It seemed ages before he spoke.

'My father and both my grandfathers had fought in a war
and I thought that this war in Vietnam was my turn to go.'

'I thought the war would be exciting and that nothing bad would happen to me. I didn't think I would get hurt.'

'Did you get hurt?' I asked.

'Oh yes, but not as bad as some of my friends. I hurt my leg there, but some of my friends were hurt much worse than me. Some of them died in Vietnam.'

I felt tears coming into my eyes.

'That's horrible,' I said, trying not to cry.

'Yes,' said Grandpa. 'But it was always horrible over there. It was so hot, the jungle was hard to walk through and we knew this was not like other wars.'

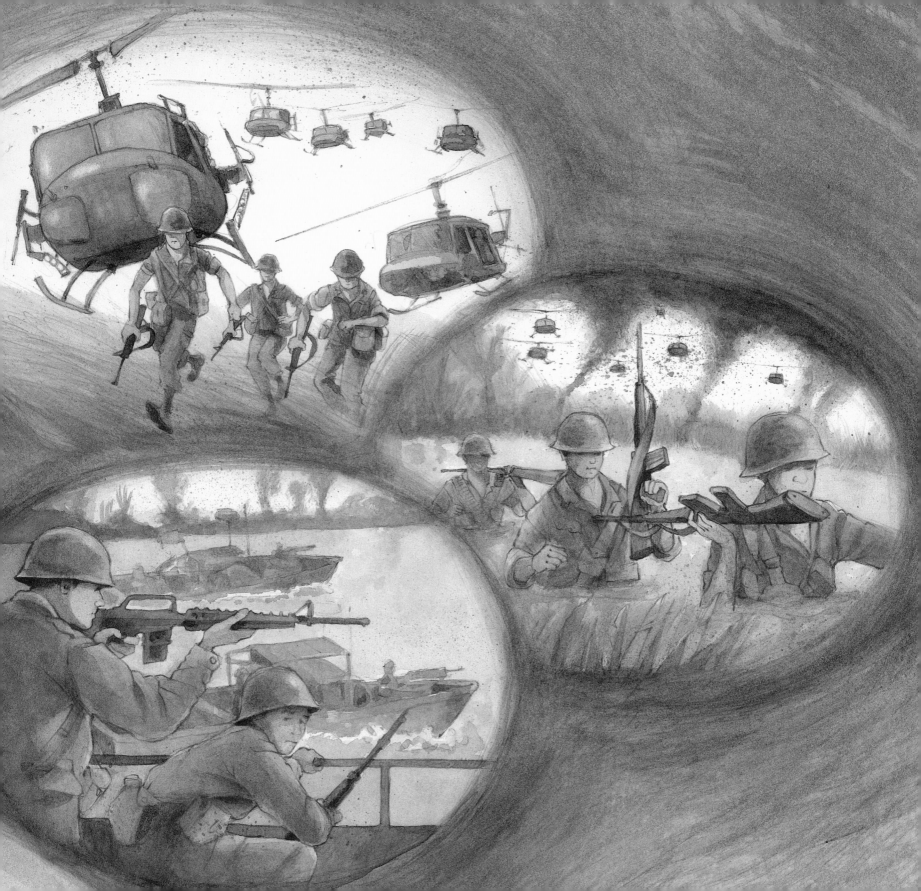

'The people there did not like us. They wanted us to leave. We were not really fighting the war for them. And we all knew we couldn't win this war.'

'Is this what makes you sad?'

'Yes, but I feel sorry for my friends who were killed or hurt. And when we came home no one thanked us for going to the war. They just wanted us to go away. Then a lot of us started to get sick from all the chemicals that had been used. Not just us; but our families too. Some people have been so sick they can't walk any more. Some have even died.'

I was so sad now that I started to cry. I looked at Grandpa's face and could see there were tears in his eyes too. I put my arms around him and said, 'I am sorry you went to that horrible war and I am sorry I made you sad, Grandpa.'

Grandpa stroked my hair
and then went to his room.

Later, Grandpa asked me to come into his room. On the table was a set of six medals.

'I got these for military service, Sarah. This one,' he said, pointing to the bronze medal at one end of the row, 'is my Vietnam Service Medal.'

The medals were bright and shone in the late afternoon sun. They looked beautiful.

'I've never seen you wear them, Grandpa,' I said.

'Here you go,' Grandpa replied, pinning the medals on the left side of his chest and smiling at me.

At that moment I felt very proud of my grandfather.

Grandpa still gets sad but now I understand why.

The Vietnam War

For all the countries involved in it, the Vietnam War was the longest military conflict of the twentieth century. The United States first sent military personnel to Vietnam in 1961. At first this commitment was small; just a few dozen specialist troops, but after the US Senate passed the Gulf of Tonkin resolution in August 1964, the number of US service personnel escalated. By 1966 there were around 200,000 US service personnel in South Vietnam and in 1969 this number had reached 550,000. Australia first sent its soldiers to Vietnam in 1962 but substantially upgraded its commitment in 1965. Nearly 60,000 Australians served in the Vietnam War. New Zealand committed 3890 military personnel between 1964 and 1972.

While both the USA and Australia committed substantial numbers of naval and air force personnel to the conflict, for most involved the war in Vietnam was fought by infantry soldiers. These soldiers spent a lot of their time on patrols in the dense jungle or conducting cordon and search operations of villages. Large-scale military actions which had occurred often in other wars were uncommon in Vietnam. Other military personnel to serve in Vietnam were engineers, artillery, sailors, medical staff, pilots and soldiers of the Special Forces.

It was a costly war too for those involved, especially for the Vietnamese people. The table shows the casualties for the USA, Australia and New Zealand:

	Fatal casualties	Wounded
USA	58,220	153,303
Australia	521	3000
New Zealand	37	187

The cost to those who survived the ordeal was also high and continues to this day.

The people from the USA, Australia and New Zealand who served in Vietnam have lived with a bitter legacy ever since. They had been fighting in a war that became very unpopular. Upon their return, many Vietnam veterans felt that the government and the public of their countries were ashamed of them. Many veterans also experienced physical and psychological health problems as a result of their service in Vietnam, for which they received little or no help. Many Vietnam veterans believe that they received no recognition for serving their country with distinction in a tough and dirty war which most people wanted to forget. They deserve better than this.